TO:

From:

GROSSET & DUNLAP
Penguin Young Readers Group
An Imprint of Penguin Random House LLC

To find out more about Eric Carle and his books, please visit eric-carle.com
To learn about The Eric Carle Museum of Picture Book Art, please visit carlemuseum.org

ISBN 9780515158069

10 9 8 7 6 5 4 3 2

THANKS

from The Very Hungry Caterpillar

Eric Carle

Grosset & Dunlap
An Imprint of Penguin Random House

Thanks

for showing me . . .

to be **Kind**
to every creature,

to **care**

**for the trees
and sky and oceans,**

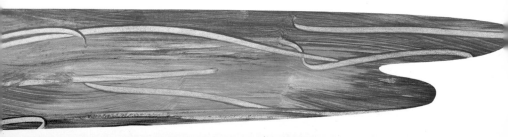

to be curious, gentle,

and **brave.**

Thanks

for reminding me . . .

to **wonder**
about everything

and to

dream

of a peaceful world.

Thanks

for encouraging me . . .

**to be a good
friend,**

to

my own song,

and to always reach

for the stars.

But most of all . . .

THANKS
for being
YOU!